Date Due			
OCT 6			
SEP 0 4 2002			

Mischa Damjan
Ralph Steadman

THE FALSE
FLAMINGOES

Scroll Press, Inc.,
New York

for Suzannah

Adebar, the stork, enjoyed life very much. Unfortunately his wife Adebaria did not. She had been quarrelsome for weeks.

"It's no fun at all being a stork," she used to say. "Nobody takes any notice of us nowadays, nobody! And what do we eat for our meals? Frogs, mice and blind-worms! Ugh!"

Adebar thought of the delicious frogs. He did not understand his wife. He shook his head.

"You smell the smoke coming out of the chimneys, don't you? In the good old days there was a smell of burnt wood; but today it stinks of petrol and oil . . ."

This time Adebar did not shake his head. This time Adebaria was right.

"Times are bad indeed! Who still believes that we protect the house we're nesting on from lightning and misfortune? Nobody! They won't even believe that we are the ones who bring the children . . ." She sighed and suddenly started flapping her wings. She went for a leisurely flight.

She flew over fields, rivers and forests, mountains and valleys. But when a town came into sight Adebaria dived down. She landed on a huge chimney. It was the chimney of the monkey's house in the Zoo.

Adebaria looked down. She saw an elephant. "Oh no," she said, shaking her head, "being an elephant is even worse: thick legs and a rough skin. Ugh!" Then she spied a rhinoceros. But again she shook her head. Then a lion roared. "I wouldn't care to be the lion either," she thought. "Leo is a king, it is true, but he's only safe in his cage. A funny sort of king!"

Still dissatisfied Adebaria turned her head to the left. And there she saw something wonderful, something fairy-like . . .

Flamingoes! "Oh!" she cried. "Oh, how wonderful!" There was a green garden with a pond in it, and there they were, the beautiful flamingoes. Some of them stood idly on one leg; some were wading in the pond, their beautiful pink bodies reflected by the clear water; some were preening their feathers, tenderly, as if they were afraid of damaging them.

There were men, women and children, standing and watching and admiring the wonderful birds.

"Oh!" Adebaria said again. "Oh!" She was completely overwhelmed by such beauty. Then she got into a panic: she nearly burst with envy. She clenched her beak and flew home.

After a very fast flight home Adebaria landed on her chimney. She had hardly arrived there when she began to rave about the flamingoes. Again and again she told her husband about the rosy birds and it looked as if she would never be able to stop.

But Adebar interrupted her: "I'm hungry, Adebaria," he said. "I must have half a dozen frogs at least."

Oh, how common this sounded. "Half a dozen frogs," she repeated to herself with distaste. Suddenly a great longing seized her. She said: "I want to be a flamingo."

"Stop this nonsense, do you hear me?" Adebar said in a very severe tone.

Nevertheless, the following day and the day after, Adebaria could not talk about anything but her longing to become a flamingo. She made Adebar feel anxious; he realized that his wife was completely possessed by the idea.

One morning Adebaria said that she would rather die than not become a flamingo. She did not eat any more, she did not chatter any more, she did not fly any more over the fields and the forests. Although spring had come and the days were growing bright and mild she did not even want to build the nest with Adebar!

When Adebar saw this he was really frightened. "How do you think you can possibly turn into a flamingo?" he asked. "It's impossible. A stork is always a stork; and a frog is always a frog," he said very wisely.

A few days later Adebaria said to Adebar: "I've found out how to become a flamingo. We have to fly to the Red Sea, have a bathe there and wish fervently to turn red . . ."

Adebar shook his head.

One day, however, when he saw how sick Adebaria was, he decided to humor her, for he not only liked delicious frogs; he dearly loved his Adebaria.

The following day they started flying southwards in the direction of the Red Sea. They knew the way well as they went by that route every year when they moved to Africa for the winter.

Hardly had they arrived at the Red Sea when they plunged into the water. And soon they made their flight back—as red birds.

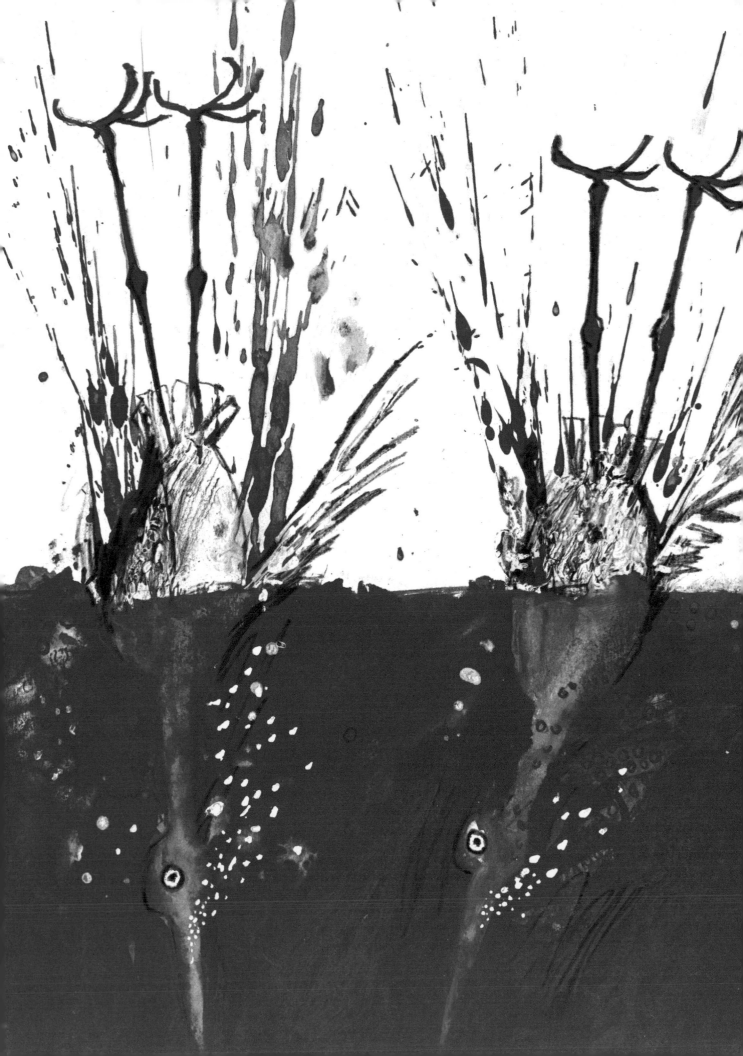

They were flying over the desert. Adebaria was happy and very proud of their color. Adebar, however, thought they had become too red to resemble the flamingoes.

"Oh, we are special flamingoes coming from some distant island somewhere in the ocean," Adebaria said, still very happy. "The important thing now is the way we behave, the way we preen our feathers. We have to be careful about what we eat. And we must get used to standing on one leg and sleeping at the same time."

Adebar thought to himself: "I shall sleep exactly as I please. Nobody will come and find out whether I sleep like a stork or a flamingo. But what about the afternoon nap?"

Adebaria was completely happy. She could not be worried by anything. She was convinced that everybody at home would admire and envy her.

After they had got home Adebar and Adebaria flew to the high chimney in the Zoo. From there they watched the flamingoes: the way they stood, moved, ate, slept. And when they were sure they knew everything a flamingo must know they flew to the pond where the storks of the region used to gather. They did not join the ordinary storks, however, but landed on the far side of the pond.

Adebaria was balancing on one leg and looking round very proudly. Adebar got annoyed because he was not allowed to eat a delicious frog. He was looking for weed and grubs of insects and worms and snails, exactly as a flamingo would have done; but deep down inside he began to regret that he had yielded to Adebaria's wishes. Adebaria did not seem to regret anything. On the contrary, there she stood, her head raised as if she were the queen of all the flamingoes.

The storks on the other side of the pond, however, did not think her a queen; they laughed at the strange couple.

"Never mind, Adebar," Adebaria said, "they're really sick with envy."

Thus the days went by and the weeks. Adebaria enjoyed helping to build the nest. And before long there were five beautiful big eggs to be seen in the nest! With Adebar's help she sat on them and eagerly looked forward to seeing her young flamingoes.

Oh yes, her joy was so enormous that she went round telling everyone that she was going to have flamingo-children. All the storks in the neighborhood smiled at the news and waited for the young birds to hatch. They were counting the days—one, two, three, four, five . . . and when thirty-three days had gone by some of them went to the nest. They had hardly got there when the young birds began to tap on the shells, and soon they emerged from the eggs: five black and white stork babies!

This made the onlookers really laugh. Adebaria was so deeply ashamed that she tried to hide her face on Adebar's breast. Now, for the first time, she repented of her wish to become a flamingo.

When the young storks had grown up and become skilled flyers there came the most grievous moment for Adebar and Adebaria: they had to say good-bye to their children who were to fly to Africa with some experienced bachelors—as is the custom among storks.

"I hope we'll see them again all right," Adebaria sighed. She suddenly had the frightening thought that they themselves might not be allowed to take part in the flight to Africa because they were neither storks nor flamingoes. Thinking all this over she repented even more that they had turned into flamingoes.

A few weeks only after the departure of the young storks Adebar and Adebaria saw from the top of their chimney that innumerable storks had gathered on a large field and that the strongest and cleverest among them was examining the rest to ensure that they were all fit for the journey. When Adebaria realized that they had to pass a test she was very frightened. Adebar was frightened too. They felt themselves neither flamingoes nor storks. And this, you will agree, is a dangerous state.

Despite their fear Adebaria and Adebar flew down to the field—for they must try to go with the others. They joined the longest line; they even hid behind a tree hoping that nobody would pay any attention to them.

Unfortunately, however, the storks' inspector had a very penetrating look and so discovered them at once.

"What's the matter with you?" he asked. "You can't come with us. This flight is for storks only!"

Hardly had he finished his sentence when he spread his wings—and all the storks, all at the same moment, rose from the ground high into the sky. They were off to Africa.

Adebar and Adebaria were the only two to remain on the field. There they stood, sadly watching as their companions left them, thinking of their children—although they were not born flamingoes they naturally loved them deeply.

Leaves fell from the trees. Winter came, and with it the bitter frost.

Adebar and Adebaria were sitting on their chimney completely lost and shivering with cold. They were resigned to death.

Without children life was not fun at all. And there was the fact, too, that they were neither flamingoes nor storks. Their beaks were chattering so loudly, however, that they caught the attention of the inhabitants of the little village. And before they had had time to turn into red icicles the fire brigade arrived, rescued them and took them to the Zoo.

There was a keeper in the Zoo who knew everything about birds. When he saw Adebar and Adebaria, however, he was amazed. He looked at them, went round them, looked at them again and shook his head. Then he stepped forward, wetted his forefinger and rubbed Adebar's feathers.

"What's this?" he cried. "You're dyed! What's that for? And who's done it? Is this a joke?"

The keeper went for a hose and washed them down until they were white and clean. "That's better," he said, "now you're real storks again!"

When spring came Adebar and Adebaria were set free. They were very happy. They waited impatiently for autumn so that they could fly to Africa with the other storks.

When it came they stood proudly in the first row of storks waiting for the inspector and flew off with the leaders, so great was their longing for their children.

At last they found them, standing not far from a Pyramid. So everybody was happy and content. Even Adebaria!